Alex and the Butterflies

By Aubrey Betz

Illustrated by Allie Daigle

To Josephine, may you always try and where you fail, may you learn, grow, and then succeed.

To any child who has ever said "I can't," "I'm too shy," or "I'm too little," may you try, try, try until you succeed.

Alex was a brave and bold girl who was happiest when climbing high in the branches of her favorite dogwood tree or pedaling quickly down the tallest hills on her bicycle.

On sunny days, she also loved walking
to the playground with her big sister Jo
where they climbed up a creaky ladder,
ran across the rope bridge, and went fast
down the big slide.

But Alex would always watch quietly as Jo swung across the monkey bars and flew so high on the swings that her feet touched the clouds.

"I'm not big and strong enough to cross the monkey bars or fly on the swings," she would think.

One day while Alex watched and wished, two butterflies landed on her shirt just at her shoulder and fluttered their wings. For a few moments, she held her breath... until they both lifted into the air.

"Where are they going?" she wondered.

Quickly she followed them.

Under the slide, through the swings, and to the other side of the playground where they paused on a blade of grass.

With great care, Alex bent for a closer look
but then something else caught her eye.

Nearby, a row of ants were marching.

Looking closer, she realized each ant was holding a large piece of leaf high over its body and carrying it far across the ground all the way back to their home.

"Wow," Alex thought, "Even though they are little, they are very strong!"

As she continued to watch, there was a flicker of yellow in the corner of her eye. The butterflies were on the move again!

Standing, she followed their lazy route, this time meandering across the grass and just to the edge of the park near the trees.

With a flutter, the pair paused on a low branch next to a mud and twig nest.

Alex tiptoed to the branch and peeked inside. There were three baby birds!

Suddenly, the smallest bird stood on shaky legs and began to slowly spread her wings.

Stepping to the edge, she flapped once or twice and lifted several inches in the air before falling back into the nest alongside her baby brothers.

"Poor birdy!" Alex gasped, "She's too little and needs to wait until she's bigger."

She had no sooner said this than the same little bird began to pump her wings again, this time faster than before, and slowly, clumsily, she lifted into the air.

"Hurray!" Alex shouted. "You did it!" as it landed on a branch close by.

A flash of yellow meant her butterflies were off once more. Happily, she skipped after them, eager to see whatever they might show her next... but was surprised when, this time, they stopped at the monkey bars.

Pausing, Alex wished again that she were big and strong so she could fly across from rung to rung like her sister. "I'm not strong enough," she mumbled.

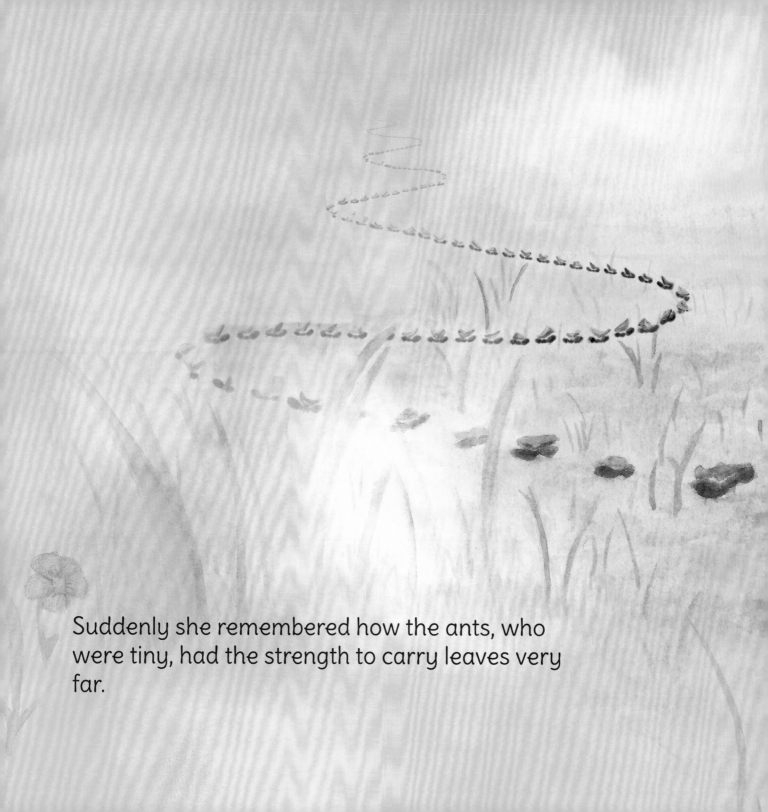

Suddenly she remembered how the ants, who were tiny, had the strength to carry leaves very far.

"Even though I'm little, I can be strong like them," she thought.

With a timid step, she pulled herself up the ladder and reached for the first rung. She stood for a moment before pushing off and swiftly moved from bar to bar, hand over hand. Halfway across, her face lit up with a triumphant smile.

She was doing it!

Thrilled with her success, Alex climbed down as she reached the other side and raced to the swings where Jo was playing.

In moments she had climbed up and was pumping her legs furiously, but the swing went nowhere.

"I can't do it!" she yelled coming to a stop with a pout.

Kicking at the rocks on the ground under her swing, she watched the butterflies go by and thought, "The baby birds, they couldn't fly the first time but kept trying until they did it."

So she decided to try again.

"Legs forward, legs back, legs forward, legs back."

With her chanting, the swing began to move, slowly at first, then faster until her toes touched the clouds and she could see all of the playground below.

Down and back up. She looked at where the ants were carrying on below and decided to always try instead of thinking she wasn't big enough or strong enough.

Down and back up. She gazed towards the tree where the little birds were learning to fly and decided to always keep trying. Even if it meant she had to start slow and practice a lot.

As their swings came slowly to a stop, Alex looked at Jo who gave her a big smile. "I knew you could do it."

Climbing down, the sisters held hands and skipped home, two butterflies flitting quietly behind.

Discussion Questions

1. Alex is happy when she's climbing trees and riding her bike. What are some activities that make you happy?
2. Did it take you a long time and a lot of practice to get good at those things?
3. Did you feel a little scared the first time you did it?
4. How did you feel after you learned how to do it?
5. Alex felt scared to try the monkey bars or swing by herself. Is there anything you are scared to try? (For example, saying "hi" to new friends at school or riding your bike without training wheels.)
6. Why are you scared?
7. Alex was scared to do the monkey bars and the swing because she thought she wasn't big enough or strong enough. Why do you think you can't do the things you mentioned?
8. Would you need help from anyone to do it? And who would you ask to help?
9. Was there ever a time you were nervous to try something but did it anyway? What happened?

Thank You to Our Kickstarter Supporters!

Heather Lantz
Wyatt Lantz
Claire Campbell
Kate Campbell
Norah Lynn Harbour
Angie Werner
Michael Wilkinson

Andrew Wilkinson
Lauren Robb
Sean Robb
Lily Jilka
Hayley Jilka
Alexandra Vollman
Josephine Vollman

Davis Brown
Cedric Brown
Sandy Heuser
Olivia Laney
Fred Kloecker
Elizabeth Kloecker
Emerson Patricia Schaefer

Author - Aubrey Betz

Aubrey Betz is a first-time author who believes in the goal-achieving power of hard work, determination, and a positive mindset. When she isn't working or playing hide-and-seek with her kids, Aubrey can be found researching genealogy, or spending quality time with her husband at their home in St. Louis, Missouri.

Illustrator - Allie Daigle

Allie Daigle is an illustrator from Connecticut who strives to create detailed and immersive images through drawing and painting. While creating artwork consumes most of her days (and nights), she always finds time for her supportive friends, family, and dog. Allie has worked on a wide array of projects-check out her website for more!

Singer/Songrwiter - Hannah McDonald

Hannah McDonald is a world-traveling musician, teacher, and songwriter with over 20 years in the music industry. She loves helping people achieve their goals and spoiling her dog Lorelei. Hannah's debut album will be released in 2021 (so the grown ups can have some songs too).

Song Link

To download your free mp3 of the song 'I Can Do Big Things' by Hannah McDonald visit:

https://aubreybetzauthor.com/product/i-can-do-big-things/

And enter coupon code "book2021". Proceed to checkout as normal. The download will be emailed to you or you can download directly from the confirmation page.

We ask that you don't share the coupon code with anyone who has not purchased a copy of the book. Thank you for supporting us!

For more information about Hannah McDonald, please visit:
facebook.com/hannahmcdonaldmusic